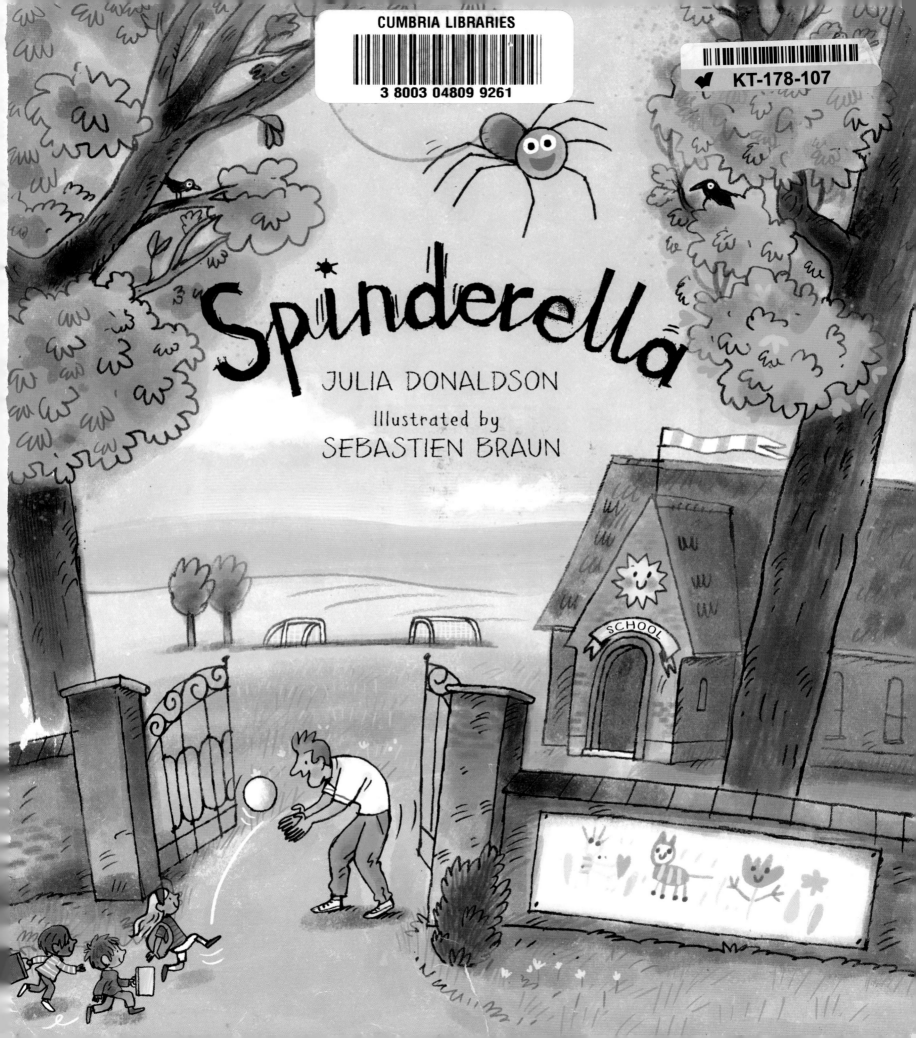

Spinderella

JULIA DONALDSON

Illustrated by
SEBASTIEN BRAUN

The children of Scuttleton Primary School were eating their dinner — fish fingers, potatoes and peas.

High up above them the spiders of Scuttleton Primary School were eating their dinner — flies, flies and flies.

"How many flies have we got today, Mum?"
asked Spinderella, the smallest spider.

"Lots," said Mum.

"Loads," said her brothers and sisters.

"That's not a number," complained Spinderella.

"Never mind about numbers. Eat up your flies," said Mum.

After dinner the children went out to play football.

The spiders swung down to watch.
"What a tackle!" they cried, and, "Yippee!"
The children scored goal after goal.

Best
Teacher
Ever

"How many goals is that, Mum?"
asked Spinderella.

"Lots," said Mum.

"Loads!" said her brothers and sisters.

Spinderella sighed. "What a family!
How will I ever learn about numbers?"

When the children had gone home, Spinderella said, "Why don't we play football?"

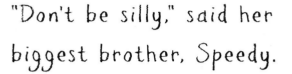

"Don't be silly," said her biggest brother, Speedy.

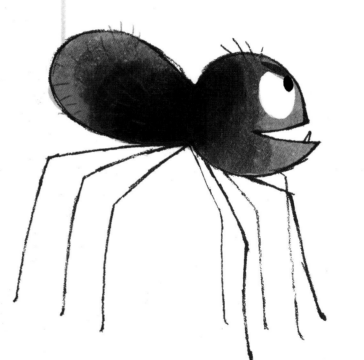

"We haven't got a ball," said her second biggest brother, Scrabble.

"I can see a pea on the floor," said Spinderella. "We can use that."

Mum chose Speedy and Scrabble
as the captains of each team.
Nearly all the spiders decided
to join Speedy's team because
he was the fastest runner.

Speedy's team scored all the goals.
"It's not fair!" the spiders on Scrabble's team shouted.

"Yes it is. You're just jealous!"
shouted the spiders on
Speedy's team.

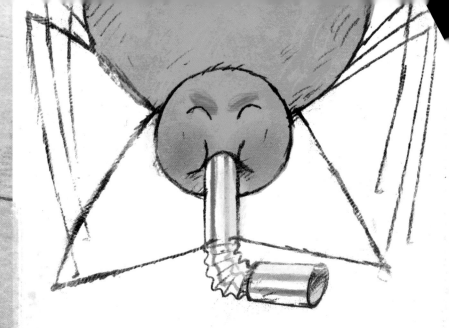

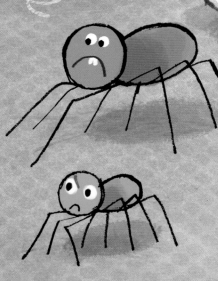

To make things worse,
the spiders hurt their
legs kicking the pea.

Before long they were all
quarrelling, moaning, and kicking
each other instead of the pea.
Mum had to blow her whistle.

"How many spiders should we have in each team, Mum?"
asked Spinderella.

"Er . . . lots," said Mum.

"Loads," said her brothers and sisters.

"I think both teams should have the same number," said Spinderella.

But her brothers and sisters all turned on her.

"Down with numbers!" they yelled.

Next morning, Spinderella woke early. She felt sad. "I wish I could learn about numbers!" she sighed.

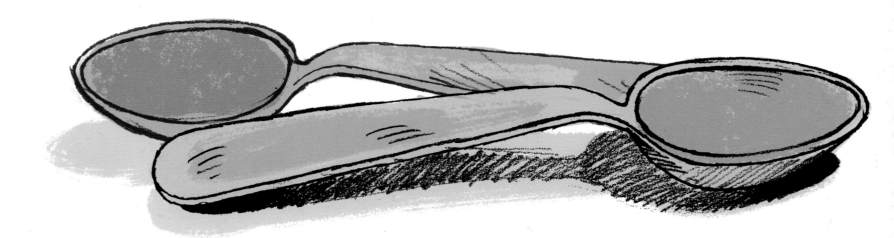

"And so you shall!"
came a loud voice.

Spinderella spun round and saw
an enormous hairy spider.

"Who are you?" asked Spinderella.
"I am your Hairy Godmother," said the enormous spider. "Follow me!"

Spinderella scuttled after her . . .

out of the dinner hall . . .

along a corridor . . .

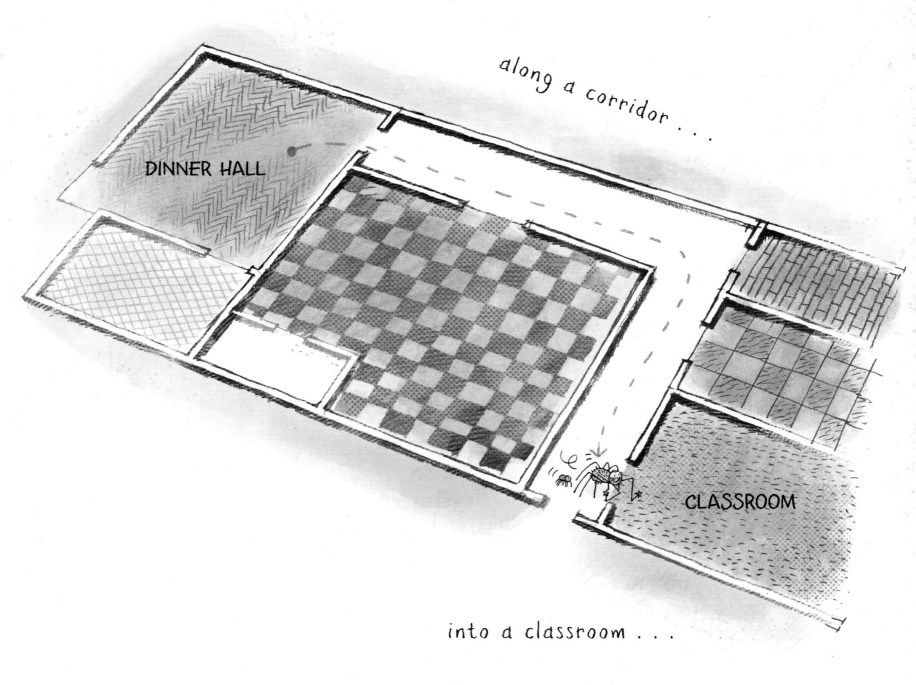

DINNER HALL

CLASSROOM

into a classroom . . .

. . . and up to the ceiling.
Spinderella looked down and saw a teacher come
into the classroom with a pile of football bibs.
"Keep your eyes and ears open!" said the Hairy Godmother,
and in a flash she was gone.

"Now, I want you to count yourselves," said the teacher. "There should be twenty of you, but let's check."

Then came the most wonderful sound. The children took turns to shout out a number, from one to twenty. Spinderella swung joyfully backwards and forwards in time to the counting.

The teacher gave out the football bibs.

"Put them on and find the others with the same colour," he said.

Soon there were two groups of children.

"How many in each team?" asked the teacher.

The children counted again.

"Ten reds," said a girl in red.

"Ten blues," said a boy in blue. "The same number!" shouted Spinderella. She was so excited that she let go of her thread.

COUNTING

"Look! A spider! Squash it!"
screamed someone.
Spinderella froze in terror.

"Let's put it out of the window,"
said the teacher, and he did.

Suddenly Spinderella was outside. "I'm lost!" she wailed. "I'll never see my mum again."

But then she turned round and spotted two football goals.
"I know where I am now!" she said.

She scuttled round the outside of the school . . .
in through the open window of the dinner hall . . .

. . . and up to the web.

"Hello, Mum! I can count
up to twenty!" she said.
"Never mind about that.
Eat up your flies," said Mum.

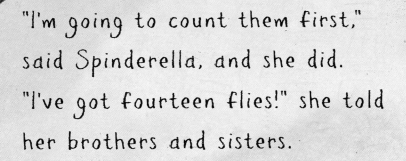

"I'm going to count them first,"
said Spinderella, and she did.
"I've got fourteen flies!" she told
her brothers and sisters.

"So what?" they said. "Down with numbers!
Up with flies and football!"

That night the spiders decided
to play football again.
"Mum," said Spinderella, "I've been
counting. There are ten of us,
so we need five spiders on each side."
Some of the spiders muttered,
"Down with numbers!"
but Mum shut them up.

Spinderella sorted them into two teams of five.
She was in Scrabble's team and she also helped
Mum to keep the score.

This time no one quarrelled or kicked each other,
and at half-time each team had scored three goals.

But still the spiders kept hurting their
spindly legs kicking the pea.
"I wish we had some football boots!"
sighed Spinderella.

"And so you shall!" came a voice.
It was the Hairy Godmother again!
"How many boots do you each need?" she asked.

"Lots," said Mum.
"Loads," said Spinderella's
brothers and sisters.

"That's not good enough,"
said the Hairy Godmother.
"I need to have a number."

"Eight!" shouted Spinderella.
"We've each got eight legs,
so we each need eight boots."
"Done!" said the Hairy Godmother.

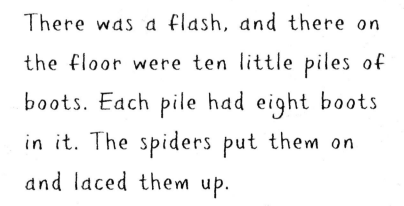

There was a flash, and there on
the floor were ten little piles of
boots. Each pile had eight boots
in it. The spiders put them on
and laced them up.

Then they had a wonderful second half. They scored goal after goal. The Hairy Godmother clapped and clapped.

With only a minute left to go, each team had scored eight goals.
"It's going to be a draw," muttered Spinderella.

But just then the ball came her way and she gave it an almighty kick.

Spinderella had scored the winning goal! All the spiders ran up to her. They picked her up, and all together then cheered, "Up with Spinderella! Up with numbers!"

To Steyning Primary School - J.D.

To Leo and Kate for their hard work,

and Tiffany for her constant support! - S.B.

EGMONT

We bring stories to life

First published in Great Britain 2016 by Egmont UK Limited
The Yellow Building, 1 Nicholas Road, London W11 4AN

www.egmont.co.uk

Text copyright © Julia Donaldson 2016
Illustrations copyright © Sebastien Braun 2016

The moral rights of the author and illustrator have been asserted.

ISBN 978 1 4052 8272 7 (paperback)

ISBN 978 1 4052 7988 8 (hardback)

A CIP catalogue record for this title is available from the British Library.

This year they decided to grow:

lettuces,   radishes,   carrots,   tomatoes,

sunflowers,   peas,   and turnips.

In early spring the children prepared the ground
by digging and raking the soil.

Later in the spring, when there was no danger of frost, they planted the seeds.

In the summer the children fed and watered the plants.

And pulled out all the weeds.

When the children came back, after their summer holiday,

they found that all the fruit and vegetables had grown.

But when they saw the turnip, they could hardly believe their eyes! It was taller than a giraffe, and wider than an elephant.

When Miss Honeywood had recovered from the shock, she asked, "How are we going to get the turnip out?"

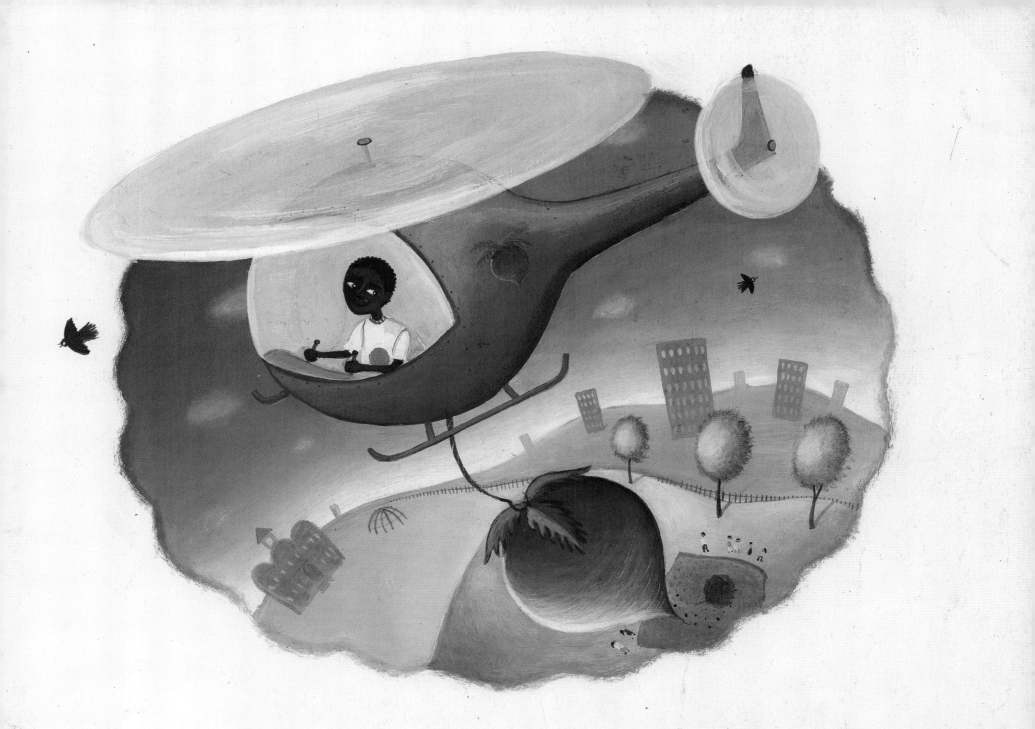

"I know, we could get a helicopter to pull it out," said Kieran.

"Or we could get a crane to lift it," suggested Tariq.

"Or a bulldozer to dig it up," said Kate.

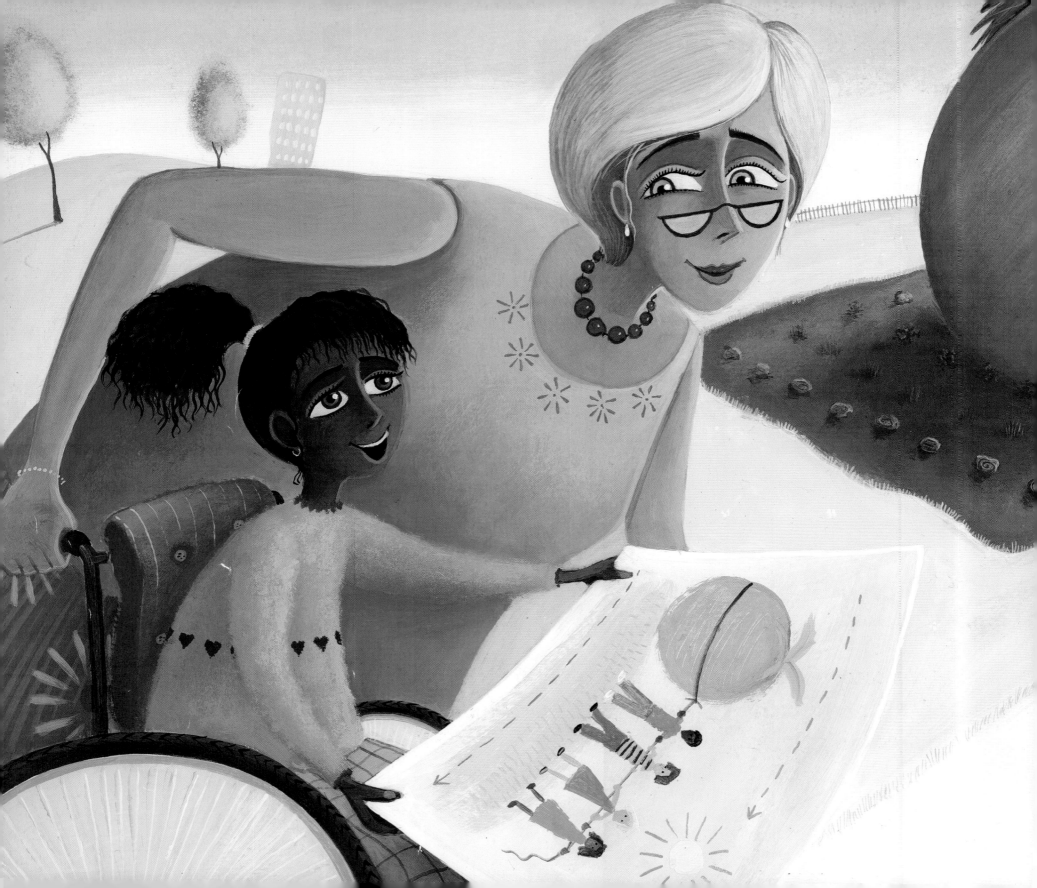

"We could tie a rope around it and all pull together," suggested Samira.
"That's a good idea," said Miss Honeywood. "Lee and Michael,
go and get the long rope."

The children tied the rope around the enormous turnip.

The boys grabbed the rope first.

They pulled and pulled with all their strength, but nothing happened.

"We're stronger than the boys!" shouted the girls and they grabbed the rope.

They pulled and pulled with all their strength but still the turnip would not move.

"Let's all try together," suggested Miss Honeywood.
"On the count of three."

"One, two, three!" shouted the children and they
all pulled together.

But the turnip still would not move.

Just then Larry arrived.
"Larry!" shouted Tariq. "We need your help!"

Larry ran to the end of the line and grabbed the rope.

"One, two, three!" shouted the children and they all pulled together.

The turnip wobbled this way and that, and then it slowly moved.
They pulled even harder and at last the turnip rolled out of its hole
and onto the grass.

The class cheered and danced around with joy.

The next day for lunch
Miss Honeywood's class
had the biggest turnip
feast ever,

and there was enough
left over for the whole
school.

To Mum, Dad, Maggie & Ben
H.B.

For Sushila
R.J.

First published in 2001 by Mantra Lingua Ltd
Global House, 303 Ballards Lane
London N12 8NP
www.mantralingua.com

A CIP record for this book is available from the British Library